Published by Lead Life Press, a division of The Lead Life Institute, LLC
St. Charles, IL

Publisher's Cataloguing-in-Publication Data
Décosterd, Mary Lou.

Magical Max makes friends / by Mary Lou Décosterd. -- St. Charles, IL : Lead Life Press, 2005.

p. ; cm.
ISBN: 0-9762408-0-7
Summary: A developmental children's book featuring a sweet little puppy who teaches kids about attitude, patience and tolerance.

1. Friendship--Juvenile fiction.   2. Individuality--Juvenile fiction.
3. Patience--Juvenile fiction.   4. Toleration--Juvenile fiction.
5. Puppies--Juvenile fiction.   6. [Friendship].   7. [Dogs].   I. Title.
PZ7.D436 M34 2005   2004114241   [E]--dc22   0502

Printed in Italy
09 08 07 06 05 • 5 4 3 2 1

For more information about the Adventures of Magical Max book series, please visit our Web site:
www.adventuresofmagicalmax.com

Magical Max
Makes Friends

Mary Lou Décosterd, Ph.D.
Illustrated by Mark Cooper

LEAD LIFE PRESS, St. Charles, Illinois • Printed in Italy

This book is dedicated to my
real-life Max, the sweetest little
puppy and my best friend.

This is Max. Max is a fluffy white puppy with big black eyes and a big black nose. Max is a special puppy who loves making friends. You'll see that Max is very good at making friends and that there is something magical about him.

One day, Max was in his flower garden and was sniffing the beautiful flowers. They smelled so good and felt so soft against his nose. All of a sudden, he heard a buzz. He stuck his nose close to the buzz, and it buzzed louder.

He stuck his nose farther into the flower bed, and when he did, he felt a tickle on his nose!

BUZZZZZZZZ

Max jumped back. "What was that?" he wondered, when out from the flowerbed came a great big bumblebee! Max had never seen anything like it before. He looked closely at the bee, did not move a muscle, and thought, "What would it be like to meet such a creature?" He decided to give it a try.

"I am Max," Max exclaimed.

The bumblebee was looking straight at Max.

Max was filled with excitement. He stayed very still and smiled, and as he did, he noticed that something strange was beginning to happen.

Max could feel his whole body begin to tingle. Then he felt his neck getting warmer and warmer.

The bee noticed something too. Max had a magical glow all around him.

The glow began to fade, but as the bee looked into Max's eyes, she knew that he wanted to be her friend. Finally the bee spoke: "Hello, Max! I am Nellie. I live here in the flower garden."

Max and Nellie began to play as they moved from flower to flower until it was time for Max to go inside.

"Bye, Nellie," said Max. Nellie buzzed close to Max and tickled his nose. Max knew it was Nellie's way of saying good-bye. He smiled happily about making a new friend.

Max's backyard looks out over a lake, and on that lake live two swans. Day after day, Max watched the swans and hoped that some day he could meet them.

One day, lo and behold, the swans came out of the water and headed toward him. As the swans got closer, they appeared bigger and bigger.

Max got excited and barked loudly.

    The swans stopped, turned, and waddled back to the lake. Max stood there, looking quite sad. He realized his barking had scared them off.

The next morning Max saw the swans. Once again, they were heading his way. Max sat quietly at the edge of his patio. This time he thought, "I will not scare them off."

The swans came over the fence to get a closer look. Max remained quiet and still. The swans came closer, and as they did, Max's body began to tingle. He was getting warmer and warmer just as he did with Nellie.

The swans saw Max's magical glow! They fluffed up their feathers and quacked with excitement.

"I am Buster, and this is Gracie," said one of the swans in a deep, loud voice.

"I am Max," Max replied.

"You are an interesting fellow, Max," said Buster as he and Gracie turned and headed back to the lake.

A few days passed. Max was outside and was lying in the grass. The sun felt so warm and cozy. He was drifting off to sleep when he heard a sound. "MEOW!"

"Hmm," he thought. Max knew that sound. That was the sound of a cat. He looked and saw a big tan cat with long fluffy fur in the yard next door. But that wasn't all.

Max heard a noise in the bushes, and out came a second cat, this one brightly colored with striped fur. "I have two cats for neighbors!" Max thought. "I don't think cats like dogs very much. I wonder what I should do!"

Max thought long and hard. He had made friends with a bumblebee and with two swans. Surely he could make friends with two cats as well.

Max smiled. The cats came closer, circled around him, and sniffed and purred. Their sniffing and purring seemed strange to Max, but once again his magical glow appeared.

The cats were amazed. They had never seen anything like it before.

"I am Butterscotch," said the tan cat. "And I am Jellybean," said the other. "You are not like other dogs. You know how to act, and we like your glow," said Jellybean.

"Thanks," Max said proudly.

That night Max drifted off to sleep and dreamed of Nellie's buzzing, Gracie's and Buster's quacking, and Butterscotch's and Jellybean's sniffing.

He dreamt about how different his new friends were. How strange they seemed at first, but they really weren't so strange after all.

Yes, indeed, Max liked making friends that were all special in their own ways. It made making friends a great adventure. Max fell deep asleep. He was excited about the new adventures that lay ahead!

Magical Max

Friendship Lessons

Max learned some valuable friendship lessons from Nellie, Gracie, Buster, Butterscotch, and Jellybean that he wants to share with you.

1. Max's first friendship lesson was from Nellie. Nellie taught Max that friendship starts with a friendly attitude. When you meet a new friend, be sure to show your best friendly attitude.

2. The second friendship lesson was from Gracie and Buster. Gracie and Buster taught Max that making friends takes patience. Sometimes you have to get to know your new friends a little at a time.

3. The third friendship lesson was from Butterscotch and Jellybean. Butterscotch and Jellybean taught Max that being a friend means appreciating the differences in others. New friends may seem strange at first, but once you get to know them you'll see they aren't so strange after all.

Magical Max Makes Friends
About the Author and the Real-life Max…

Mary Lou Décosterd is a developmental psychologist who has worked with children and families for more than 20 years. She has worked on numerous projects promoting children's emotional health and well-being including her latest heartwarming book series, The Adventures of Magical Max. The series is inspired by the antics of the author's Westie, Max.

Max, now four years old, has shown himself to be a remarkable puppy, opening up his heart and soul to all around him. Max has a true zest for life and an uncompromisingly positive nature, making him a wonderful friendship role model for children of all ages.

About the Illustrator...

Mark Cooper is an award-winning illustrator and art director in both print and film making with more than 20 years of experience in the United States and overseas. Mark is currently founder and owner of Quick-Draw Creative Group in Orlando, Florida.